ORCA
Echoes

BRUNO for REAL

CAROLINE ADDERSON

illustrated by HELEN FLOOK

ORCA BOOK PUBLISHERS

Library and Archives Canada Cataloguing in Publication

Adderson, Caroline, 1963-
Bruno for real / Caroline Adderson ; illustrated by Helen Flook.

(Orca echoes)
ISBN 978-1-55469-023-7

I. Flook, Helen II. Title. III. Series: Orca echoes
PS8551.D3267B78 2009   jC813'.54   C2008-908028-9

First published in the United States, 2009
Library of Congress Control Number: 2008943123

Summary: This is the second collection of stories about Bruno, an imaginative boy
with a humorous personality.

Orca Book Publishers gratefully acknowledges the support for its publishing programs
provided by the following agencies: the Government of Canada through the Book
Publishing Industry Development Program and the Canada Council for the Arts, and the
Province of British Columbia through the BC Arts Council
and the Book Publishing Tax Credit.

Typesetting by Teresa Bubela
Cover artwork and interior illustrations by Helen Flook
Author photo by Caroline Adderson (self-taken)

ORCA BOOK PUBLISHERS
PO Box 5626, STN. B
VICTORIA, BC CANADA
V8R 6S4

ORCA BOOK PUBLISHERS
PO Box 468
CUSTER, WA USA
98240-0468

www.orcabook.com
Printed and bound in Canada.
12 11 10 09 • 4 3 2 1

For the very real John Fernando

Contents

Good Night, *Hic Hic*

Bruno tried all the tricks, but he still couldn't get to sleep. He tried counting sheep. One, two, three, four, five…Five little sheep came over the green hill. They looked like clouds with legs. One, two, three, four, five…Five little sheep rolled down the other side. *Wheee!* What fun! They rolled faster and faster. At the bottom, they all landed in a wooly heap. But not for long. They jumped right up and ran to the top of the hill again for another roll. *Wheee!*

Now Bruno was even less sleepy. He tried a different trick. He closed his eyes and pretended his bed was a boat. It was a rowboat floating in the water. The boat rocked from side to side.

Bruno yawned. He was getting sleepy—very, very sleepy. Then he opened one eye. The boat was speeding down a river! It was heading for a waterfall!

Wheee!

"Mom!" Bruno called. "Mom! Mom! Mo-o-o-m!"

Mom peeked in the bedroom door. She looked really sleepy. "What is it, Bruno?"

"I can't get to sleep."

"That's because you're yelling. Good night," she said.

"I wasn't yelling!" Bruno said. "Mom? Mom!"

Mom came back. "What is it, Bruno?"

"I wasn't yelling," Bruno said. "I was calling."

"All right, all right," Mom said. "Try counting sheep."

"I did!" Bruno said. "It was too much fun!"

"Okay. Try singing a little song," she said.

"Then I'll be singing," Bruno said. "How can I get to sleep if I'm singing?"

"Never mind," Mom said. "Good night."

Mom went back to bed. Bruno lay in the dark for a while. Then he got up to use the bathroom. When he got back to his room, he tucked in all his stuffed animals. He hopped into bed. Then he got up again to check the lid on his box of pencil shavings. Yesterday the box had spilled all over the floor. Dad got mad. He'd wanted to vacuum up Bruno's collection of pencil shavings!

Bruno lay in the dark. "Sleep?" he whispered. "Sleep? Where are you?"

Sleep said, "*Hic.*"

Bruno sat up. "Sleep?"

"*Hic.*"

But it wasn't Sleep talking. It was Bruno. Bruno had the hiccups.

"Mom!" Bruno called. "Mo-*hic!*"

This time Dad came. "Bruno! Pipe down!"

"I can't sleep. I've got the *hic.*"

Dad brought Bruno a glass of water. "Drink this," he said. "It should do the trick."

4

Bruno drank all the water. He gave Dad the glass and said, "Thank *hic*."

Dad sat on the bed. "Okay. Here's another trick. Hold your breath for as long as you can."

Bruno took a deep breath. He counted in his head. One, two, three, four, five…He counted all the way to forty-seven. Then he gasped for air.

"Very good," Dad said.

"*Hic*," Bruno said.

"Do you know it's eleven o'clock?" Dad said. "Mom's already asleep."

"I can't *hic* it," Bruno said.

"I know. But I'm tired and want to go to bed myself. Here's one more trick. Stand on your head."

Dad turned on the bedroom light. Bruno got down on the floor and put his head on the carpet. Dad lifted Bruno's ankles in the air. Bruno was standing on his head! He looked around the room. It seemed funny that the books on his bottom shelf were on the top shelf now. The floor was the ceiling,

and the ceiling was the floor. Bruno felt like an astronaut! His head grew heavy, and his feet grew light. His head was filling up with blood. It was getting bigger. And BIGGER! Soon he wouldn't be able to get his shirts on! Soon his head would be too BIG for the neck hole!

"Stop!" Bruno cried.

Dad let go of his ankles. Bruno tumbled to the floor. "*Hic!*"

"Okay," Dad said. "Okay. I know one last trick. It's the very last one."

"What?"

"BOO!" Dad said.

Bruno looked at Dad. "Why did you say that?"

"I was trying to scare your hiccups away."

"That wasn't scary at all," Bruno said. "*Hic.*"

"What would scare you?" Dad asked.

"Nothing. I'm not scared of anything."

"Monsters?" Dad asked.

"No. But the hiccups would probably get scared if something jumped out at them in the dark."

So Dad went to hide while Bruno, *hic*, counted to ten. Then Bruno tiptoed out of his room. He crept down the dark, dark hall and into the dark, dark living room so they could scare the hiccups away.

Dad jumped out from behind a chair. "BOO!"

Bruno wasn't scared. Neither were his—

"*Hic!*"

"I give up," Dad said. "Let's both go back to bed. The hiccups will get bored and go away."

Bruno went to bed. *Hic. Hic. Hic.* It seemed that his hiccups wanted to talk. "It's time to go to sleep," Bruno told his hiccups. "Pipe down."

"*Hic.*"

Now Bruno got mad. He was so mad he got out of bed and went to his parents' room to complain. He opened the door and looked in. Mom was sleeping. Dad was snoring. Bruno tiptoed over to the bed. He leaned over Dad.

"*Hic.*"

Dad screamed!

Mom screamed!

Bruno screamed!

That did the trick.

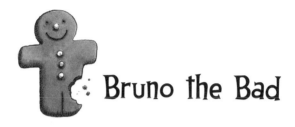 Bruno the Bad

One morning Bruno woke up bad. "I'm bad," he told Mom at breakfast.

"You mean you're in a bad mood," she said.

"No. I'm just bad. Listen."

He cackled. "Ah-ha-ha-ha-ha!"

He growled. "Grrrr."

And he wrinkled his nose. This made a little horn of skin grow between his eyebrows.

"Stop," Mom said. "You're scaring me. I can see your horn."

"You should be scared," Bruno said. "Because I'm bad! I'm Bruno the Bad!"

Mom poured Bruno a glass of orange juice. "I don't want orange juice," Bruno the Bad said. "I want a glass of blood."

She really looked scared then. Bruno guessed she was glad when it was time for him to go to school.

He wasn't very bad at school because he didn't want to get in trouble. But at recess, on his way out to play, he stopped at the principal's office. Bruno's principal, Mrs. Foss, always left her door open. She looked up from her desk. "Can I help you, Bruno?"

Being sent to the principal's office was the very worst thing that could happen at school. Bruno put one foot in the door. Then he ran off. Mrs. Foss laughed.

At lunch, Bruno found a gingerbread man in his lunch box. He thought of another bad thing. He could eat his cookie *before* he ate his sandwich.

"Ah-ha-ha-ha-ha!" he cackled.

"No!" the gingerbread man cried. "Don't eat me! Don't! Please!"

Bruno said, "Ginger, this is the end of you!"

Isabel was eating her lunch across the table from Bruno. She looked scared. "I'm telling!" she said. And she put up her hand and called out to the teacher, "Ms. Allen! Bruno's talking to his cookie!"

Everyone laughed!

That night, Bruno told Mom how he had been to the principal's office. He didn't say that Mrs. Foss had laughed or that his class had laughed.

"Did you do something wrong?" Mom asked.

"I was bad," Bruno told her.

"I think Mrs. Foss would have phoned me," Mom said.

"I was bad all day," he said. "I did something really, really bad. I did the worst thing I've ever done."

"What did you do?" she asked. Bruno could tell by her voice that she was afraid of finding out.

"I ate the arms and legs off my gingerbread man *before* I ate his head."

"You *are* terrible," Mom said. She leaned over to kiss him good night.

"No kisses!" Bruno yelled. "I'm bad!"

Mom sat down on the bed. "No good-night kiss, Bruno?"

"No!"

"How about when I drop you off at school?"

"No!"

"No kisses when you hurt yourself?"

"No kisses ever!"

She pretended to cry. Bruno knew she wasn't really crying, but he still felt bad. He felt bad, and he *was* bad! He was Bruno the Bad!

He went to his dresser and got a mitten. "Here," he said. "Kiss this."

Mom kissed the mitten. Bruno took it back and rubbed it all over his face.

"What about me?" she asked.

Bruno kissed the mitten. Mom left with it pressed to her heart.

The next day, Bruno found the mitten in Mom and Dad's room. He packed it in his backpack. "Why are you taking the mitten to school?" Mom asked.

"I don't want you kissing it when I'm not here," Bruno told her.

After school, Bruno watched the other kids get picked up. Some kids let their moms and dads kiss them. But they were *good* kids. Bruno was *bad*. He'd done a few more bad things that day, like writing his name backward on his work.

"Who's Onurb?" Ms. Allen, his teacher, asked.

"Grrrr!" Bruno said.

She looked scared. "Who let a bear in the classroom?"

Bruno loved being bad. Dad enjoyed it too. One night Mom went out and left Bruno and Dad at home alone. "Okay," Dad said, rubbing his hands together. "This is our chance. Let's be as bad as we want."

"Grrrr!" Bruno said.

For dinner, Bruno and Dad had macaroni, but they didn't use a fork or spoon. They ate it with their hands! After dinner, they took out all of Bruno's puzzles and mixed the pieces up. They put them all together as one giant mess. It looked terrible! It looked awful! "This is the baddest puzzle ever," Bruno said.

Dad agreed. "It's the worst."

Then, at bedtime, instead of a good-night kiss, Bruno gave Dad a good-night bite.

Being bad with Dad was the best!

The last day Bruno was bad, he hid in the closet. When Dad came home and hung up his coat, Bruno jumped out of the closet growling and showing his horn. He jumped right on Dad's back. Dad ran with him to the living room. They wrestled on the couch. "Grrrr! Grrrr!"

Whoops! Bruno tumbled off the couch and hit his head. "Ow!"

Now he *really* felt bad.

"Mom!" he yelled.

She came running. "What happened? My poor baby! Let me get the mitten!"

"No!" Bruno wailed, holding his head. "I think I need a kiss!"

The Long Birthday

When Bruno turned seven, he invited twelve pirates to his party. He wore a pirate scarf and an eye patch. He drew sword slashes on his arms and face. Instead of real blood, he bled jam. Dad made a birthday cake in the shape of a treasure island.

As soon as the other pirates arrived, they had a sword fight. "Be careful! Please be careful!" Mom said. But only one pirate got hurt, and he didn't even bleed.

"We need more jam!" Bruno called.

Next they had a treasure hunt. Dad gave them a map made from a paper bag. He wrinkled it so it looked old. It was a map of the backyard.

They found the treasure and ate it. It was chocolate coins. Then Bruno blew out the candles on the treasure island, and they ate that too.

Bruno got lots of presents, even a real treasure chest filled with colored stones. Everyone walked the plank. Afterward, the parents of the tired pirates came to pick them up.

That night Bruno told Dad, "Today was the best day of my life."

"I'm glad you had fun. You only turn seven once in your life."

"I wish every day was my birthday," Bruno told Dad.

At breakfast the next morning, Bruno told Mom, "Today is a very special day."

"Is it?" Mom said.

"Yes. Today I am seven-and-one-day old. Did you know you are only seven-and-one-day old once in your life?"

"I've never looked at it that way," Mom said. "What should we do about it?"

"I think we should bake a cake," Bruno said.

Mom said she was too tired after yesterday's party. "Why don't I put a candle on your pancake?"

Mom lit the candle on Bruno's pancake. Bruno made a wish and blew the candle out. He wished that it could be his birthday every day. But he didn't tell Mom his wish. He wanted it to come true.

The next day was Monday. "Happy birthday to me, happy birthday to me," Bruno sang.

"What?" Dad said. "Is time moving backward?"

"No," Bruno said. "I'm seven-and-two-days today!"

"How wonderful!" Dad said.

"Can I stay home from school?"

"No," Dad said.

When he got to school, Bruno told his teacher that he was seven-and-two-days. Ms. Allen pointed to the calendar. "Class, today Bruno is seven-and-two-days old. How old will he be on Friday?"

"Seven-and-six-days," someone said.

"Very good! And how old will he be next Wednesday?" Ms. Allen asked.

They talked about Bruno's birthday for a long time. Bruno was happy until he realized they were doing math. He put up his hand and said, "If we talk about this any more, Bruno will be dead."

Every night Bruno gave himself a birthday present. He put one of the stones from his treasure chest under his pillow. In the morning, he looked under the pillow to see what he had got for turning seven-and-three-days, seven-and-four-days, and seven-and-five-days. At dinner, Mom and Dad sang "Happy Birthday" to Bruno. Mom put a candle in his bun. She put a candle in his peach. She put a candle in his soup.

"What's floating in my soup?" Bruno asked.

When Bruno turned seven-and-eleven-days, Mom and Dad sat him down for a talk. "There are 365 days in a year, Bruno," Dad told him. "You can't have 365 birthdays."

Bruno said, "Why not?"

Mom said, "Because there aren't any candles left."

So they stopped singing "Happy Birthday." For a while, Bruno remembered to put a stone under his pillow. Soon he lost count of his age. Was he seven-and-twenty-two-days or seven-and-twenty-four-days?

When Bruno was about seven-and-twenty-six-days old, he noticed Mom looked sniffly. "Are you crying?" he asked.

"Yes, I am," she said.

"Why?"

"Because I'm forty today!"

Bruno knew it was her birthday because he and Dad had gone out to buy her a special present. "What's the matter with forty?" Bruno asked.

"It's old," she said.

"You're right," Bruno said. "But two hundred is older."

Mom laughed and blew her nose.

"Don't you want your birthday?" Bruno asked.

"No," she said.

"Can I have it?" Bruno asked.

Mom thought this was a great idea. She baked a cake for Bruno. That night, Dad made a special dinner. Mom and Dad sang "Happy Birthday" to Bruno. Before he blew out the candles, Bruno asked, "What about the present?"

"It's yours," Mom said. "No birthday is my present."

Bruno closed his eyes and made a birthday wish. He wished that when he opened the present, it wouldn't be a frilly nightie. The wish came true, of course. Birthday wishes usually do.

"A pirate scarf!" Bruno cheered.

He tied it around his head.

Bruno Makes a Deal

Bruno got home from school hungry. He was so hungry he fell down on the kitchen floor. Dad emptied Bruno's lunch box. "No wonder you're hungry," Dad said. "You didn't eat your sandwich."

"There was green in it," Bruno said.

"Then why didn't you swap it?"

Bruno sat up. "Swap? What's *swap*?"

"You know—trade," Dad said. "When I was a boy, I always swapped the things I didn't like in my lunch."

"For what?" Bruno asked.

"For a better lunch."

Bruno said, "I'll swap you my green sandwich for some macaroni."

"It's a deal," Dad said.

The next morning, Mom made Bruno's lunch. Bruno asked her to please, please, please put lettuce in his sandwich.

"Call nine-one-one!" Mom shouted. "Quick! We need an ambulance!"

But she did what Bruno asked. She sent him to school with a very green sandwich.

At lunch, Bruno opened his lunch box and took the sandwich out. He looked around at what all the other kids had. Some of them had green in their sandwiches too. But some of them were eating sandwiches Bruno liked: cheese sandwiches, ham sandwiches, ham-and-cheese sandwiches. His friend Ravi had something even better.

"Is that a macaroni sandwich?" Bruno asked Ravi.

Ravi said, "Yes."

"Is it good?"

"Yes. But I've had macaroni sandwiches for three days in a row."

"I'll swap you," Bruno said. He showed Ravi the inside of his sandwich: ham and butter and six pieces of lettuce. They took the sandwich apart on the desk. They counted all the leaves.

"That's not dirt," Bruno told Ravi. "That's pepper."

"It's a deal," Ravi said.

The macaroni sandwich was good. It was so good that the next day Bruno asked Mom for a macaroni sandwich. It was his favorite sandwich now. At lunch, he didn't want to swap it.

But after he ate the macaroni sandwich, he was too full to eat his cookie. He went up to Ms. Allen's desk. "Ms. Allen? Would you like this cookie?"

Ms. Allen smiled. "Aren't you sweet, Bruno."

"I want to swap it," he said.

"Oh." Ms. Allen's smile went away. "All right then, Bruno. What do you want to swap it for?"

Ms. Allen's pencil sharpener was on her desk. It was one of Bruno's favorite things in the classroom. It was electric and whirred so loudly that everyone jumped when a pencil got sharpened. It also had a window that showed all the shavings inside. Bruno asked to trade the cookie for the pencil shavings.

"That cookie," Ms. Allen said, "for those pencil shavings?"

"Yes," he said.

"It's a deal, Bruno."

Bruno collected pencil shavings. When he got home from school, he added his class's pencil shavings to his collection. The box was nearly full!

He was so happy he looked around for other things to swap. He found an eraser shaped like a heart in his toy box and plastic teeth under his pillow. The teeth had been there for a long time. The tooth fairy was probably never going to come. And he had three of the same hockey cards!

The next day was very busy. When you are busy, the day goes by very fast. Usually school lasted forever. Today school lasted a minute and a half. Already, Bruno was back home eating supper with Mom and Dad.

"Where did you get that funny hat?" Mom asked him.

"I swapped for it," Bruno told her.

Dad looked proud. "Did you? What did you swap?"

"I swapped Mom."

Mom put down her fork. Her face turned white.

"Don't worry," Bruno told her. "I got you back."

Dad said, "Thank goodness! I like your mother."

"Me too," said Bruno. "I like her so much I swapped my plastic teeth to get her back again."

"Plastic teeth?" said Mom. "The pointy ones?" Now her face turned very red.

"Yes," Bruno told her. "First I tried a pickle. No deal."

"I hope not!" Mom cried.

"What were you doing with a pickle?" Dad asked. "You don't eat pickles. They're green."

Bruno said, "I swapped for it."

"What did you swap?"

"A huge bug I found at recess."

"Now that's a deal," Dad said.

"It was dead," Bruno said.

"Even better!" Dad patted Bruno on the back.

The hat had flaps over the ears. Strings hung from the flaps. If Bruno wanted to hear better, he tied the strings in a bow on the top of his head. He showed his parents how it worked. "For math, I put the flaps down. For recess, I put them up."

"Well," Mom said, "it's hardly school anyway. It's more like a swap meet."

The doorbell rang. Mom and Dad looked at each other. "Who is that?"

"Ravi's dad," said Bruno. "Ravi traded him. I have just the hockey card he needs."

Bruno, Level 5

On the last day of swimming lessons, Bruno had to take a test. He had to show the teacher what he'd learned. He showed her his flutter kick. He showed her his side glide. He showed her his back float. Bruno could float on his back for a very long time. He was an excellent floater.

"That's great, Bruno!" the teacher called.

Bruno kept on floating.

The teacher called, "Bruno? Bruno?"

Bruno floated on.

"Hello, Bruno? You can stop floating now!"

"Hey," Bruno told her. "You woke me up!"

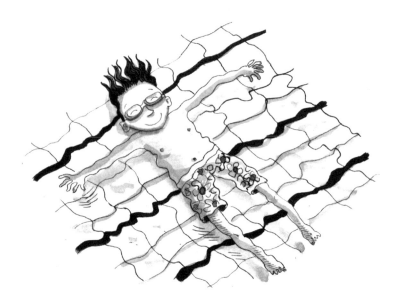

Next he showed her his rollover glide with flutter kick. Bruno added two extra rollovers. "That was a screwdriver glide with flutter kick," he said.

The last thing Bruno had to do was swim from one side of the pool to the other. Mom came and cheered him on. "Yeah, Bruno!" she called. When he got to the other side, Mom was there again. "Bruno! Bruno! Rah, Rah, Rah!" Bruno was a little bit embarrassed. All the other parents were sitting on the benches like they were supposed to.

Afterward, the teacher handed out the report cards. A badge was stapled to Bruno's card. It read: *Swim Star 2.*

"You did it!" Mom cried. "You passed! You're in level three now! You really are a Swim Star!"

Mom was so happy. She was happier than if she'd passed level two herself. But she hadn't. She couldn't swim at all. At the cabin in the summer, Mom usually stayed on the beach. Sometimes she went in the water up to her knees. She always said, "I'm more of a wader than a swimmer."

"Swimming is easy," Bruno told Mom as they were leaving the swimming pool. "Watch." And he swam all the way across the parking lot to the car.

"Easy for you," Mom said. "I sink."

"You sink?"

"Yes."

"Then I think I know what your problem is," Bruno told her. "I think you have rocks in your bathing suit."

Back home, Bruno noticed that things looked different now that he was in level three. The bathroom sink was lower. Also, the toothpaste was easier to reach. "When you are at a higher level, everything looks lower," he told Mom and Dad.

Even bending over to tie his shoes was different. "Hello down there!" he called to his shoes. They seemed so far away. They looked lonely. He knelt down to tie them so they wouldn't feel so alone.

Bruno asked Mom to sew his swim badge on his coat. The next day at recess, he showed everyone. "Now I'm in level three."

"Then why is there a number two on the badge?" Isabel asked. She wasn't a Swim Star, Bruno could tell.

"You get the badge when you finish a level," Bruno explained. "I finished level two."

His teacher, Ms. Allen, was standing nearby. She asked him if he had a badge for level one.

"I do," Bruno said. "But I put it somewhere safe. I put it somewhere so safe that I can't find it."

"When you do find it," Ms. Allen asked, "will you sew it on your coat?"

"No," Bruno said. "I can't sew."

"All right," Ms. Allen said. "But if you did have both badges on your coat? How much would they add up to?"

Bruno turned and ran away. That Ms. Allen! She was always sneaking in the math!

The bell rang and Bruno went back in the school. He did the math. He tried not to, but he couldn't help himself. In the classroom he told Ms. Allen, "Three. They would add up to three."

"You're a Math Star," Ms. Allen told him.

Now Bruno really wanted to find his level one badge. If Mom sewed his level one badge next to the level two badge on his coat, they would add up to his level—level three. He looked in all his drawers. He looked under his bed. He looked in his piggy bank.

"Where's my level one badge?" he called.

Mom came into his room. "This badge?" she asked, pointing to it. Bruno was using his level one badge for a bookmark.

Mom sewed it on his coat for him. "See?" Bruno showed her when she was done. "One plus two is three. I'm in level three."

"And you're only in grade two!" she said proudly.

"That's right. I'm in level three in swimming and grade two in school. Three plus two is five. That means I'm really in level five."

"Level five in what?" Mom asked.

"In life."

"No!" Mom cried. "I want a little boy a little longer!"

At dinner that night, Bruno cut up his meat himself. Usually Dad cut it for him, but now that he was in level five in life, he did it himself. When he finished drinking his milk, he went to the fridge to get the jug. He poured out another glass for himself. Mom or Dad used to do that for him, back when he was in level two.

"Level five in life?" Dad said. "It seems like only yesterday you were in level one."

Mom sniffed and wiped her eyes with her napkin.

"I remember being in level five," Dad said.

"Really?" Bruno asked. "What did you do when you were in level five?"

"That was when I started eating things that were green."

Bruno looked around the table. Luckily, Mom and Dad had already finished all the salad. It was safe for him to say, "Yes, I'll eat green now that I'm in level five."

"And level five was when I started washing the dishes."

"Really?" Bruno said. "Level five? That sounds more like level eight."

Dad shook his head. "That's level five."

After dinner, Dad filled the kitchen sink with water. He added dish soap and put all the dirty dishes in. Then he called for Bruno—Bruno, level five in life.

Bruno started washing. Mom came and stood next to him. She said, "How's my little boy?"

Bruno said, "Help! I'm sinking!"

He was sinking all the way back to level three!

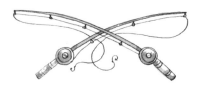

School of Boys

Summer holidays came. No school for two months! Bruno and his mom and dad packed the car to go to the cabin. They brought books and fishing rods, swim goggles and sleeping bags. They brought cards, an air mattress, and the blue-and-white-striped sun umbrella.

When they got to the cabin, the first thing Bruno did was run down to the dock. Last summer they rented this same cabin. Last summer there were fish. He lay on his tummy at the end of the dock and looked into the ocean. The fish were still there! A *school* of fish. Bruno had moved up to the next level in his swimming lessons. He hoped the fish had too.

Mom, Dad and Bruno unpacked their things. Bruno had a new sleeping bag he wanted to try out. But the zipper was tricky. It was very, very long. "This zipper is six miles long!" Bruno complained. "I can't get it up."

Mom showed him how. He got in the sleeping bag and zipped it closed right over his head. Then he unzipped it and got out. He never had a problem with the zipper after that.

Bruno ran out of the cabin to help Dad make a fire. There was a stove in the cabin, but a campfire was more fun than using pots and pans.

"I need newspaper crumpled into balls," Dad said. "And lots of small sticks."

Bruno got the newspaper and made balls. He ran around collecting sticks. Dad chopped the firewood with the ax. Then he showed Bruno how to make a little tepee of sticks over the newspaper. "After the sticks get going, we can add the firewood," said Dad.

Bruno finished building the stick tepee by himself.

"We need one more thing," Dad said.

"What?"

"Matches!"

Bruno ran to get them.

That evening they cooked their hot dogs and broccoli and marshmallows on sticks around the fire. They heard a loud honking in the sky. It was Canada geese flying over the cabin, just like last summer.

"The school of geese!" Bruno shouted.

"It's not a school," Dad said. "It's a *flock*."

"It's a *gaggle*," Mom said.

"It's a flying school," Bruno said.

Mom and Dad laughed.

They were still laughing about the school of geese the next morning. Mom had noticed ants on the picnic table carrying her toast crumbs away. "Bruno," she said. "Here's a school of ants. What are they learning?"

Bruno watched them for a few minutes. Most of the crumbs were bigger than the ants. "Weight lifting," he said.

Bruno loved being at the cabin. There were so many different kinds of animals. There were birds, fish, snakes, seals, starfish, deer. Some of these animals didn't go to school. They had already learned to be snakes and deer. Others still needed lessons. Like the dragonflies. One day, they had a picnic on the beach. Mom said, "Look!" Dragonflies filled the air. They had green bodies and papery wings that whirred.

Just then a helicopter flew over. "There's the teacher," Bruno said.

The starfish were learning how to hug underwater. When the tide went out, Bruno climbed on the rocks to count them. They were purple and pink and uncountable. But they could hug. He couldn't pull them apart no matter how hard he tugged.

The seals were learning clapping songs in the bay. They swam in as the sun went down and had their lessons there. In his sleeping bag at night, Bruno could hear their flippers slapping the water.

His friend Ravi arrived with his family. They rented the cabin next door for two weeks. Ravi and Bruno fished and played hide-and-seek. They swam all day.

Bruno spent almost the whole summer at the cabin, but it wasn't long enough. "I don't want to go home," he said.

"We have to go back to work," Mom told him. "And you have to go back to school."

"We need to buy your school supplies," Dad said. "That should be fun."

It was true. Bruno liked to go to the store at the end of the summer and pick out new pencil crayons.

New pencil crayons meant more shavings for his collection. "Can I get new pencil crayons even if I don't go back to school?" Bruno asked.

"If you don't go back to school?" Mom asked. "What are you talking about?"

That summer Bruno had caught three fish. He'd learned to zip up a sleeping bag with a six-mile zipper. He and Ravi had built a fort. One night they were allowed to sleep in it. Bruno could make a fire all by himself. He wasn't allowed to, but he could.

Bruno didn't think he needed to go back to school. He had already learned all he needed to be a boy.

In *Bruno for Real*, the sequel to *I, Bruno*, award-winning author Caroline Adderson shares more of Bruno's really real adventures. Caroline lives in Vancouver, British Columbia, with her husband and the son who lied to her when he said he'd always be seven.